STORMY NIGHT

By Hubert Flattinger

Illustrated by Nathalie Duroussy

Translated by J. Alison James

North-South Books

NEW YORK/LONDON

Copyright © 2002 by Nord-Süd Verlag AG, Gossau Zürich, Switzerland
First published in Switzerland under the title *Wenn du glaubst du bist allein . . .*
English translation © 2002 by North-South Books Inc., New York

First published in the United States, Great Britain, Canada,
Australia, and New Zealand in 2002 by North-South Books,
an imprint of Nord-Süd Verlag AG, Gossau Zürich, Switzerland.

Distributed in the United States by North-South Books Inc., New York

Library of Congress Cataloging-in-Publication Data is available.
A CIP catalogue record for this book is available from The British Library.
ISBN 0-7358-1666-2 (trade edition) 10 9 8 7 6 5 4 3 2 1
ISBN 0-7358-1667-0 (library edition) 10 9 8 7 6 5 4 3 2 1
Printed in Germany

For more information about our books, and the authors and artists
who create them, visit our web site: www.northsouth.com

If the night is dark and wild,
If the booming thunder wakes you,

If the windows shake and rattle,
And the shadows prowl the walls,

If something in the attic stirs
And rustles over dusty floors,
That's the time to think of me,
And all will be well.

If the curtains float like ghosts,
And a cold wind chills your toes,

If the lightning shocks the night,
So the tree is bright with blue,
That's the time to think of me.
That's the time I'll think of you.

If your teddy hides his eyes,
And the toys all cringe in fear,

If you can't quite brave the floor,
And you can't quite find the door,

Even if each step you take

Makes the floorboards creak and shake,

Still it's right to come to me,

For all will be well.

If a giant twisting snake

Lies in wait beside the stairs,

If the slippery-fingered rain
Tip-taps on the windowpane,
And if every single tap
Makes your heart
Feel like stone,

If you feel you're all alone,

That's the time to come to me.
On my lap and in my arms,
I will hold you safe and warm,
And all will be well.